BENNY'S FLAG

Phyllis Krasilovsky   ILLUSTRATIONS BY Jim Fowler

Published by ROBERTS RINEHART PUBLISHERS
An imprint of the Rowman and Littlefield Publishing Group
4501 Forbes Boulevard, Suite 200, Lanham, MD 20706

Distributed by NATIONAL BOOK NETWORK

Library of Congress Catalog Information Available
ISBN 978-1-57098-320-7

Book design by Ann W. Douden, Boulder, Colorado
Manufactured in the United States of America

Dedication

For Amy Dale, great artist, great friend, in memory
of our happy Alaskan days —P.K.

For Dale DeArmond, who gently and modestly
shows how art should be made —J.F.

Benny was an Aleut boy who
lived in Alaska many years
before it became a state.

He had straight black hair
and bright black eyes, but
best of all he had a happy
friendly smile.

He had many, many
friends in the mission home
where he lived. That was a place
for boys and girls whose families could
not take care of them.

The children ate together in a big dining room. They slept
in big rooms, called dormitories, which had many beds in
them. And in the winter they all went to the same school that
other children in the village attended.

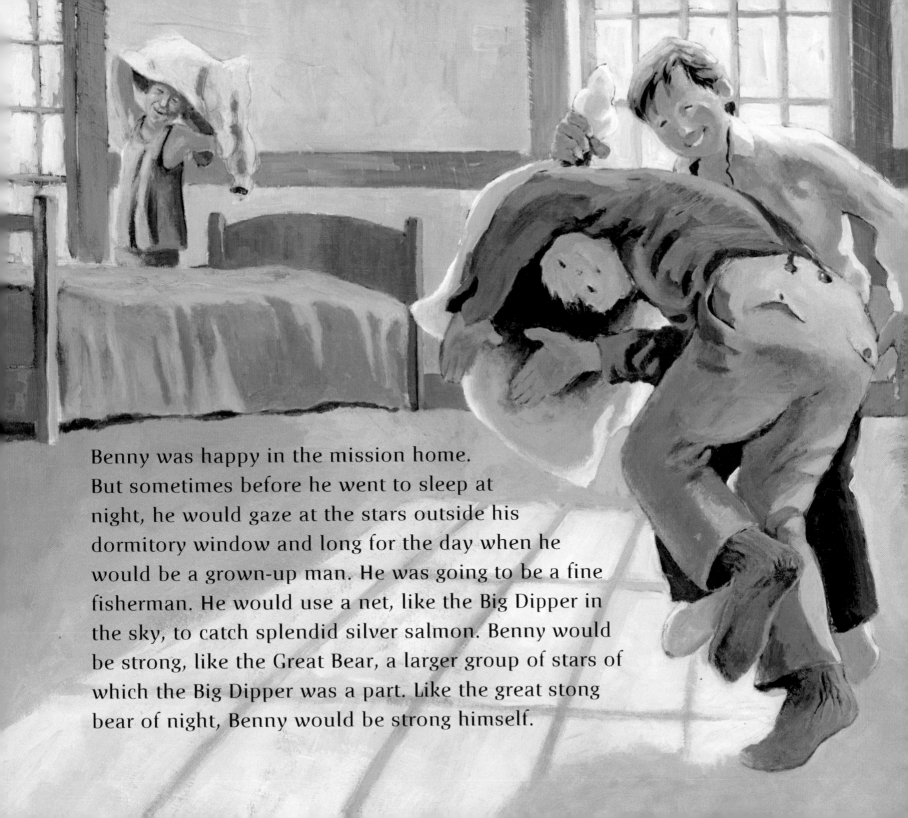

Benny was happy in the mission home.
But sometimes before he went to sleep at
night, he would gaze at the stars outside his
dormitory window and long for the day when he
would be a grown-up man. He was going to be a fine
fisherman. He would use a net, like the Big Dipper in
the sky, to catch splendid silver salmon. Benny would
be strong, like the Great Bear, a larger group of stars of
which the Big Dipper was a part. Like the great stong
bear of night, Benny would be strong himself.

The North Star would
guide his boat. Benny
knew that when Alaska
became a state someday, it would
be the northern most state in the United States.
Sometimes when the sky was scattered with hundreds of
stars, it reminded Benny of a field of forget-me-nots, the
little star-shaped flowers that grow wild everywhere. The
blue sky was a roof that covered Benny's Alaska at night.

In the summertime, when only the mountain tops were still covered with snow, Benny enjoyed himself on picnics with the other mission children. Sometimes he went swimming, too, though the water was often cold.

One lucky day a kind fisherman took Benny fishing with him in his boat. Almost at once Benny caught a big salmon all by himself. It was so big that there was enough for everyone at the mission house to eat for supper, and everyone said it was delicious.

Benny was so happy he could hardly sleep that night. He lay awake looking at the stars, dreaming his dream of becoming a real fisherman.

When fall came, school started again just as it does for children everywhere. But the winter came quickly. The first snowy day Benny went to school wearing a parka, mukluks, which are fur lined boots, and thick mittens to keep his fingers warm. He looked more like a furry bear than a boy!

As he walked along the snow-covered road, he wondered if all
the little blue forget-me-not flowers that covered the fields in
summer were now growing under the earth. In the cold winter
sunshine the world was all white-and twinkly snow. The
salmon were gone. The fishing boats, anchored near the
beach, looked like a fleet of ghost ships.

That day in school the teacher told the children that there was a contest to make a flag for Alaska. With all his heart Benny wanted to win the contest. He thought how grand it would be to see his flag carried in a parade, or hung on the masts of big ships that came to the village in the summertime. He thought how especially grand it would be to see his flag flying on the fishing boat he would have one day.

That night the boys and girls at the mission house collected crayons, paint, and paper, and made many, many designs for the flag. They sat around a big table, and as they worked, they talked and laughed and sometimes held up their designs for

the others to see. But Benny sat quietly, thinking and
thinking. For once no one could see his happy, friendly smile.
He was thinking of what he loved the most about Alaska.

Suddenly Benny knew what he wanted his flag to be like. He wanted his flag to be like the stars he dreamed by—gold stars spread out like the Big Dipper in the blue sky. So that is what he painted. And underneath it he wrote these words:

"The blue field is for the sky and the forget-me-not, an Alaskan flower. The North Star is for the future state of Alaska, the most northerly of the Union. The dipper is for the Great Bear—symbolizing strength."

Some of the children drew pictures of the beautiful
snow-covered mountains in Alaska. Some drew pictures of the
big fish that can be caught in Alaska. Some drew pictures of
the northern lights that sometimes cross the sky. Some drew
pictures of the Alaskan forests. Some drew pictures of
the Alaskan glaciers, and some drew pictures of
the Alaskan rivers. And some drew star
designs or stripe designs or flower designs.

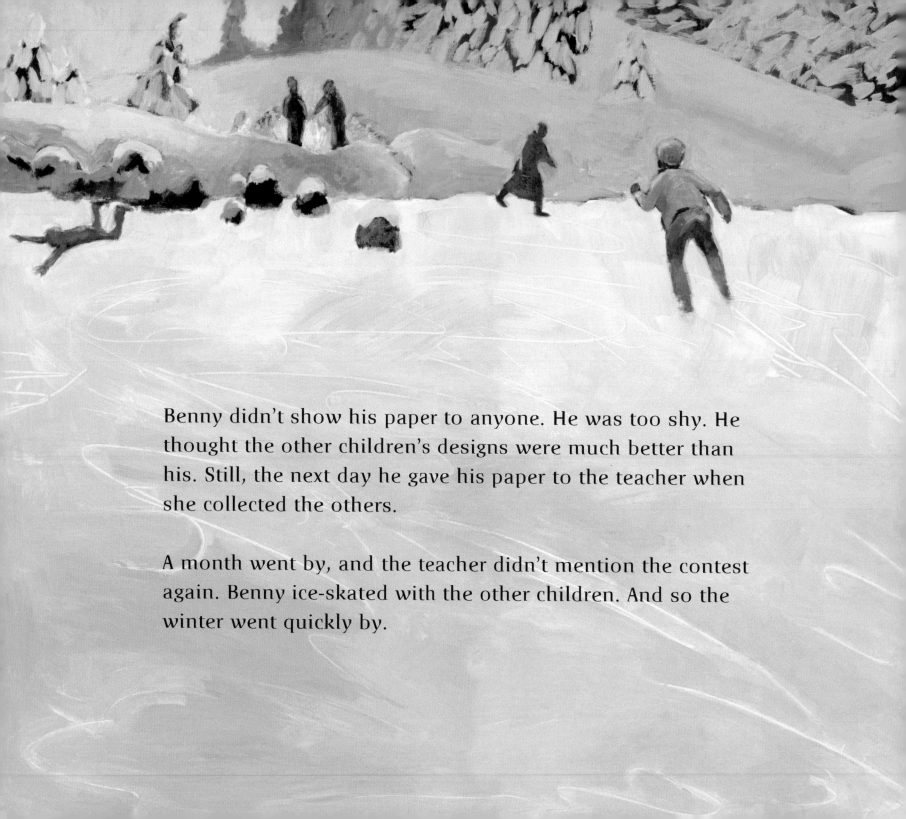

Benny didn't show his paper to anyone. He was too shy. He thought the other children's designs were much better than his. Still, the next day he gave his paper to the teacher when she collected the others.

A month went by, and the teacher didn't mention the contest again. Benny ice-skated with the other children. And so the winter went quickly by.

And suddenly the snow and ice began to melt. Benny no longer wore his parka and mukluks and mittens. He began to watch for the forget-me-nots in the drying fields as he walked to school.

He watched the fishermen mend their nets for the
coming fishing season. He watched the world change
from white to green.

Then, one day, when school was almost over, the teacher called the children together.

"Children," she said, "the flag contest is ended.

From all over Alaska boys and girls sent in
designs for the flag. From northern Nome to the
busy cities of Anchorage and Fairbanks...from the
fishing towns of Seward and Petersburg to Juneau,
the capital, and lumber town of Ketchikan...from
everywhere came hundreds of designs.

"And . . . boys and girls! Benny's design has won the contest! From now on, Benny's design will be Alaska's flag!"

What a proud and happy boy Benny was! And what an
especially proud and happy boy he was on the Fourth of July.
For on that day in the village a big parade celebrated the
holiday. Everyone came—to see the marchers in their bright
uniforms, the baton twirlers, the banners—but the very first
thing they saw was BENNY. Benny marching at the head of
the parade, carrying the flag he had made for Alaska!

This is a true story.